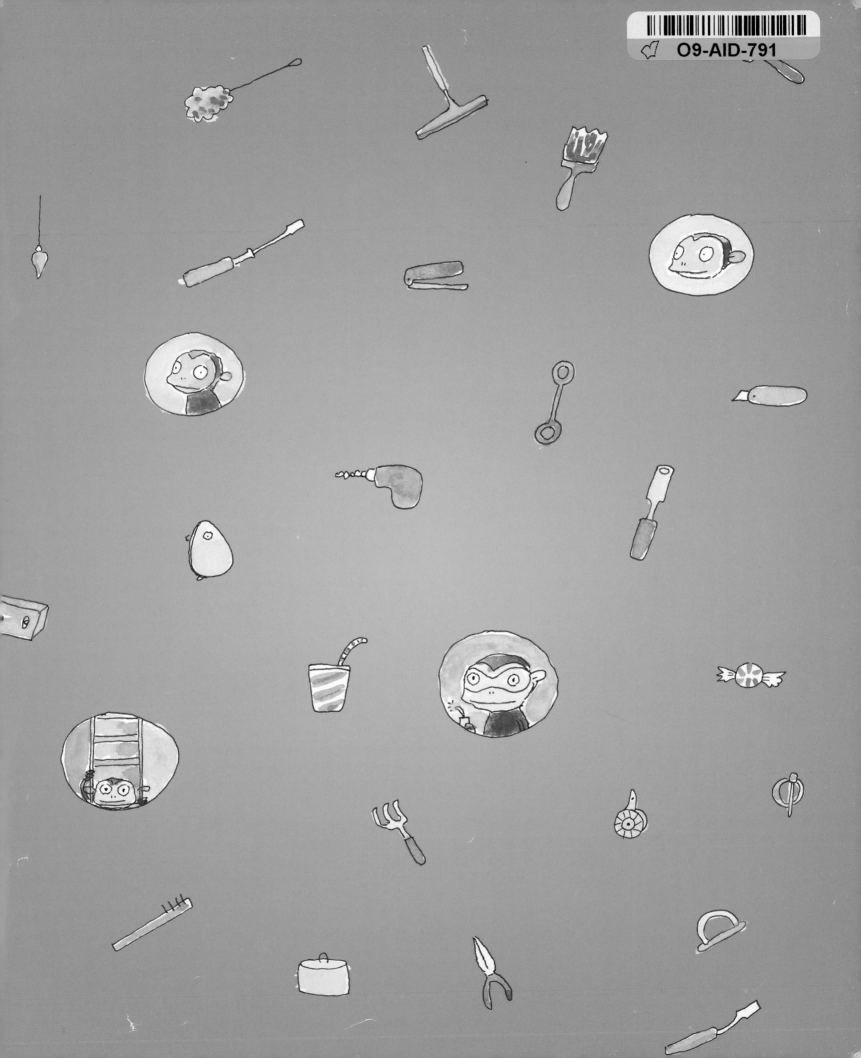

Monkey With A Tool Belt And The Maniac Muffins

Chris Monroe

CAROLRHODA BOOKS MINNEAPOLIS

To Mom

Carolrhoda Books
A division of Lerner Publishing Group, Inc.
241 First Avenue North
Minneapolis, MN 55401 USA

For reading levels and more information, look up this title at www.lernerbooks.com.

Design by Zachary Marell
Main body text set in Blockhead Unplugged 20/30.
The illustrations for this book were created in pencil on illustration board and then painted in gouache and inked.

Library of Congress Cataloging-in-Publication Data

Names: Monroe, Chris, author.
Title: Monkey with a tool belt and the maniac muffins / by Chris Monroe.
Description: Minneapolis : Carolrhoda Books, [2016] | Summary: Chico the monkey has to step in and save the day when his friend Clark the elephant's cooking nearly destroys their town.
Identifiers: LCCN 2015037490 | ISBN 9781467721554 (lb : alk. paper) | ISBN 9781467795623 (eb pdf)
Subjects: | CYAC: Tools—Fiction. | Cooking—Fiction. | Monkeys—Fiction. | Elephants—Fiction. | Animals—Fiction.
Classification: LCC PZ7.M760 Mo 2016 | DDC [E]—dc23

LC record available at http://lccn.loc.gov/2015037490

Manufactured in the United States of America
1 – DP – 7/15/16

Chico Bon Bon had never seen

a pancake do so much damage.

Clark had been making breakfast, and now the kitchen table had no legs. Dishes were broken. Syrup was everywhere. Their friend Wayne was stuck to the floor.

Clark was getting ready for the party he was throwing for Uncle Bill's graduation from hotel-motel management school.

Chico was there to help with the cooking.
He was a good cook and had many great
tools for cooking on his tool belt-apron.

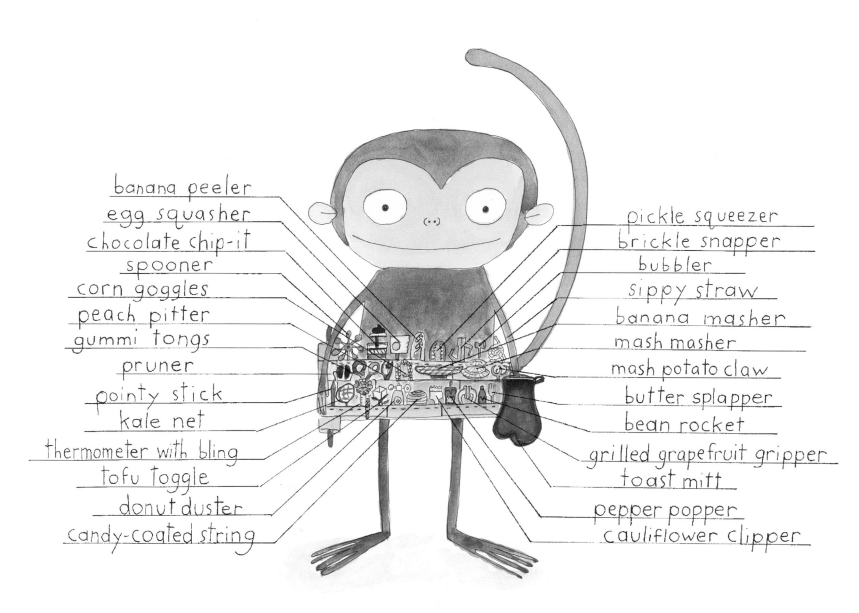

banana peeler
egg squasher
chocolate chip-it
spooner
corn goggles
peach pitter
gummi tongs
pruner
pointy stick
kale net
thermometer with bling
tofu toggle
donut duster
candy-coated string

pickle squeezer
brickle snapper
bubbler
sippy straw
banana masher
mash masher
mash potato claw
butter splapper
bean rocket
grilled grapefruit gripper
toast mitt
pepper popper
cauliflower clipper

But Chico saw other ways he could help.

The kitchen was a disaster zone.

He removed a small pumpkin,
stuck in the drain.

He rehung the pot rack
and welded the chain.

He removed some white chocolate
from Jimmy the Mouse

and gathered the meatballs
that had rolled 'round the house.

Clark's lemon pudding
had started to stew.

Chico tried stirring,
but it was like glue.

The pudding was thick,
and the spoon was quite bent.

How could lemons and sugar
make rubber cement?

He took out those pancakes to bust them apart.
He used his large winch to put them on the cart.
They were so big and heavy,
he piled them in stacks.

He'd deal with them later.
He needed his ax!

When Chico had fixed everything, he decided to start working on his famous chocolate marshmallow banana boats.

Clark was working on his supersecret blueberry muffins. Clark had memorized the recipe, and an elephant never forgets. Well, almost never. He started adding the ingredients to a huge bowl.

Chico glanced over at Clark.

That seems like a lot of baking powder, Clark.

I know this recipe so well I can make these in my sleep!

Clark finished the batter and poured it into a muffin tin. He popped the tin into the oven.

Now to work on my Egg Surprise!

Everyone was busy in the kitchen
making all kinds of treats.

RUMBLE RUMBLE RUMBLE RUMBLE RUMBLE RUMBLE RUMBLE RUMBLE RUMBLE RUMBLE RUMBLE RUMBLE RUMBLE RUMBLE RUMBLE

A few minutes later,
they heard an odd
noise coming from
the oven. It sounded
like popcorn.

Really BIG popcorn.

Then they heard a groaning sound,
then a whistling sound,
then a grinding sound,
and then, finally,
but not really surprisingly,

they heard . . .

The door BLEW OFF THE OVEN and flew straight out the window!

The muffins began shooting
out of the oven like hot
blueberry cannonballs.
Everyone ran for cover. The
muffins had really expanded.
They looked like monsters!!

They bounced around the room.

On their way toward the door,
the muffins took out

the mixer,

the sugar bowl,

two chairs,

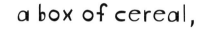

a box of cereal,

a jar of
sprinkles,

three
gingerbread men,

and the entire spice rack.

They burst out the door and smashed
down the steps, leaving crumbs
and broken concrete everywhere.
They were **SO BOUNCY!!!!**
They were **SO HEAVY!!**

They bounced down the street.

They flattened
a lawn chair.

They just missed
some hula-hoopers.

They knocked
down a fence

and
demolished
a garden
gnome.

and headed for Main Street.

Chico chased after them. They were falling apart as they bounced, but they didn't seem to care! Somebody could get hurt!

What was he going to do??

Quickly, Chico figured out a plan:

1. He ran back to Clark's house.

He finished loading the pancakes onto the cart.

2. He grabbed the lemon pudding.

And ate a peanut.

3. He pushed the cart downtown.

He ran fast.

4. He made several sawhorses with his saw, hammer, nails, and a pancake.

MAIN STREET

HATS

5. He filled a pastry bag with the gluey lemon pudding.

It was sticky but smelled delicious.

6. He glued the pancakes to the sawhorses with it.

SPWIT

Then he squeezed the pudding all over the front of the pancakes.

Then he hid.

Within seconds, the maniac muffins
bounced around the corner.

They were headed his way!!!

The muffins hit the pancakes and immediately disintegrated into crumbs.

Chico jumped out and rolled the pancakes around the crumbs.

Clark and
Chico's friends
showed up.

Clark's big-mistake pancakes and sticky lemon pudding
had saved them from his muffins.

Try this!

They all began eating the giant rollup. It was delicious!
They had created a taste sensation!!

"Hooray!!" everyone yelled, spitting crumbs everywhere.

"Oops, sorry," they all said, quickly
covering their mouths with their paws.

Clark was glad his pancakes had saved the day.

"Mistakes can be so helpful!" he said happily.

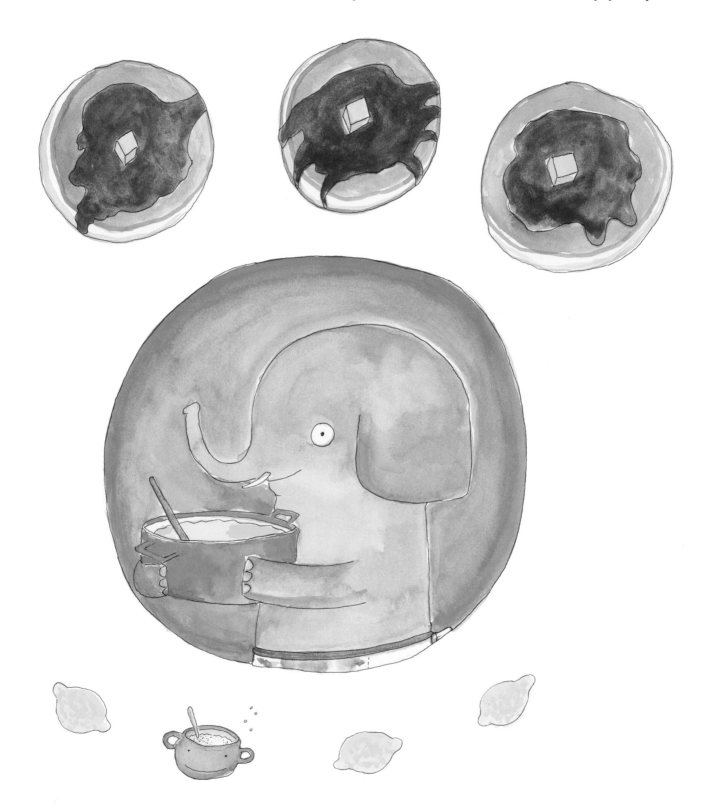

They all returned to
Clark's house, fixing
the broken things
along the way.

Although the lawn
gnome was never
quite the same.

Back in the kitchen, they all pitched in and cleaned up.

After repairing the kitchen,
they got back to cooking.
They had just a couple
of hours until Uncle Bill's
guests would arrive.

Later at the party, all the food was GREAT . . .

even though some of it was a little weird.

And everyone agreed the giant pancake lemon
muffin jelly rolls were a smashing success.

The End

BLUEBERRY MUFFINS

12 muffins

2 cups flour
¼ cup sugar
1 T. baking powder
½ t. salt
1 egg (beaten)
1 cup milk
¼ cup canola oil
1 cup blueberries

- Mix dry ingredients.
- Stir in egg, milk, oil until moistened.
- Stir in blueberries.
- Spoon into lined tin.

400° oven

20-25 minutes

BANANA BOATS

4 boats

4 bananas (peels on)
6 T mini marshmallows
6 oz semi-sweet choc. chips
4 12" squares of foil

- Cut bananas lengthwise ½" deep. Leave ½" uncut on both ends.
- Pull gently apart and stuff with chocolate and marshmallows.
- Wrap in foil.

350° oven

10-12 minutes

PANCAKES

9 cakes

Mix:
1 beaten egg
2 T melted butter
¾ cup milk

Add:
1 cup flour
1 T sugar
1 t baking powder
½ t salt

- Drop by ¼ c. spoonfuls on to hot buttered griddle.
- When bubbly on top and golden on bottom, flip. Cook about 2 more min.

Medium-low heat